Perfectly Princess

Green Princess Saves the Day

by Alyssa Crowne

illustrated by Charlotte Alder

Scholastic Inc.

New York   Toronto   London   Auckland
Sydney   Mexico City   New Delhi   Hong Kong

For my friends Alice and Amy,
who like trees and birds as much as I do.

ISBN 978-0-545-20848-2

12 11 10 9 8 7 6   11 12 13 14 15/0

Printed in the U.S.A.   40

Designed by Kevin Callahan
This edition first printing, June 2010

Contents

Chapter One

Princess of the Park

"Come here, little bird," Holly Greenwood said in a singsong voice. "I won't hurt you, I promise."

Holly was sitting quietly in her favorite spot in Peterson Park, underneath the weeping willow tree. It was cool and shady, and there was a little patch of bright yellow buttercups nearby. There were other flowers too, tall orange ones, but Holly didn't know what they were called.

Peterson Park was Holly's favorite place in the whole world. Sometimes she went there to play with her friends. But she loved to spend time alone, too. If she sat quietly under the willow tree, the animals that lived in the park would sometimes come close.

For a long time, the chipmunks were Holly's favorite. She liked their fuzzy tails and the black-and-white stripes on their golden fur. And when they stuffed their cheeks with nuts, it always made Holly laugh.

But a week ago, Holly had noticed a new animal in the park. She spotted the little bird perched on a branch of a raspberry bush. It had bright blue feathers on its head and wings, and its belly and neck were a pretty reddish brown color. It was the most beautiful bird Holly had ever seen.

Today, the bird was sitting on the raspberry bush again.

Tweeeet tweet tweet tweet tweet, he sang. *Chirp chirp chirp!*

Holly pushed her lips together and tried to whistle, like her mom had showed her. But the sound came out all messy: *pffffffft!*

Holly sighed. The princesses in her favorite stories made it look so easy. They sang a pretty song, and all of the cute forest creatures came running. Little birds even landed on their fingertips! Holly wished that would happen to her. Being friends with the park animals was the best part of being a princess—better than living in a castle or marrying a handsome prince!

"Please, little bird?" Holly asked.

But the bird flapped its wings and flew away.

"Someday it will happen," Holly said out loud. "Someday I will be just like a real princess!"

"Holly! Where are you?"

Holly jumped up and brushed the dirt off of her skirt. Her big sister, Jessica, always walked to the park with her when their mom was at work. But Jessica never wanted to stay for very long.

"Coming!" Holly called out.

She raced to the big white gazebo, where Jessica sat with her friends. Holly's brown braids bounced on her shoulders as she ran.

"Do we have to go already?" Holly asked her sister. She wanted to try one more time to get the bird to land on her finger.

Jessica rolled her eyes. "We've been here, like, all day," she said. "I don't know why you think this park is so great."

Jessica was sixteen. Holly knew she'd never understand. But that didn't stop Holly from trying to explain.

"It's the best park in the world!" she said, stretching her arms out to the sides. "It's got swings and a swirly slide and lots of trees and flowers and—"

"Okay, I didn't really want an answer," Jessica said, smiling a little. "And we can't stay, anyway. I have a science project to do."

Jessica waved good-bye to her friends, took Holly's hand, and headed down the path. Holly smiled as an orange butterfly flew past them and landed on a daisy.

When they got to the end of the path, Holly stopped. A big sign was sticking out of the grass. It said FOR SALE.

"'For Sale'?" Holly asked. "What's for sale?"

Jessica walked up to the sign. There was a lot of smaller writing on it. She read it for a minute.

"Wow," she said finally. "It looks like the park is for sale."

Holly wasn't sure she heard right. "The whole park?"

Jessica nodded. "The town is trying to sell it. They want to turn it into a shopping center."

"They can't!" Holly cried. She couldn't believe it.

Who would want to get rid of the most beautiful park in the world?

Chapter Two

Princess Power!

"**Mom, you have to talk** to Mayor Morgan about this," Holly said later that night. "She can't sell the park. She just can't!"

Holly, Jessica, and their mom sat around the kitchen table. They were eating Holly's favorite dinner, spaghetti and salad. But Holly wasn't enjoying it very much. She was too worried about the park.

"I can talk to her, but I don't think she'll change her mind," Mrs. Greenwood said.

Holly frowned. "Can't you *order* her not to sell the park?"

Her mom smiled. "Holly, I just work in the town clerk's office. I can't tell the mayor what to do."

"I wish you could," Holly said, sighing. "The mayor is making a big mistake!"

Jessica shrugged. "I don't see what the big deal is," she said. "Maybe they'll put a Pizza Town in the new shopping center. That would be cool."

"That would *not* be cool!" Holly yelled. "What will happen to all of the animals that live in the park? They can't live in Pizza Town."

Mrs. Greenwood put a hand on Holly's shoulder. "Please don't yell, Holly," she said. "We can't order the mayor to keep the park, but there are other ways to change her mind."

"Like what?" Holly asked, lowering her voice and twirling some spaghetti around her fork.

"You could write a letter," her mom suggested. "And we can spread the word about what's happening to the park. If a lot of people speak up, the mayor might listen."

Holly was quiet for a minute. Tons of ideas were jumping around in her head! She ate her last bite of spaghetti and stood up.

"I've got to get to work!" she announced.

"Dishes in the sink first, please," said Mrs. Greenwood.

Holly put her dishes away and ran to her bedroom. It was very small, but Holly didn't mind. She thought it was the best bedroom in the world.

Last year, when she turned six, her aunt Amy had painted all the walls for her. Everywhere Holly looked, she saw trees and flowers. The ceiling was blue, just like the sky. Aunt Amy had painted birds in the trees, butterflies on the flowers, and squirrels and chipmunks peeking out of the grass. Holly's mom had even gotten her a green rug, so the floor looked like a grassy field. Her room reminded Holly of being in Peterson Park!

Holly went to her dresser and picked up her favorite headband. It had tiny white

flowers and little green leaves on it. She put it in her hair like a crown and sat down on her rug. Her crown always helped her think better.

Holly closed her eyes and imagined that she was princess of Maple Grove, and that she lived in a green castle, with lots of trees around it. Instead of tearing down the park, she would build more and more parks in Maple Grove. All of her subjects would be happy.

Holly opened her eyes. She knew just what to do.

"Princess Power will save the park!" she cheered.

Chapter Three

Holly's Plan

"I need your help, Zachary," Holly said.

It was Monday, and Holly was in the lunchroom with the rest of her class. Holly and Zachary always sat next to each other. His last name was Grover, and they were seated in alphabetical order at lunch.

Holly was glad Zachary's last name began with a G. She had sat next to him ever since kindergarten. Zachary was nice.

Zachary chewed a bite of his tuna fish sandwich. "What kind of help?"

Holly pulled a stack of papers out of her green lunch bag. Her Princess Power had given her a great idea! She had made lots and lots of flyers. They all said the same thing:

Come to a meeting to
SAVE THE PARK!
Holly's house
Monday after school

"Hold on," Zachary said. He took off his glasses and wiped them with a napkin. Then he put them back on and read the flyer. "'Save the park'? What park?" he asked.

"Peterson Park," Holly replied. "The mayor wants to tear it down."

"No way!" Zachary said. "That park is cool."

"Exactly," Holly said. "That's why we need to have a meeting. We need lots of people to help save it."

"I know what we could do," Zachary said, talking fast. He always talked fast when he got excited. "We could have a big party in the park for everyone in town! We could have ice cream and play games and —"

Holly shook her head. "No," she interrupted him. "That would take too long to plan, but I have another idea. First, we need a meeting."

"Who's going?" Zachary asked.

Holly grinned and handed him some flyers. "That's where we come in. We need to invite people. Let's pass these around."

"Sure," Zachary said. "Let me just finish my sandwich."

Holly stood up. "Please, Zachary, can't we do it now?" she asked. "Saving the park is important!"

"I guess you're right," Zachary said.

He grabbed some flyers and headed for another lunch table. Holly took some to the table where her friends Grace and Taylor were sitting. The two girls looked very different. Grace had long, straight black hair and dark, almond-shaped eyes. Taylor had curly blonde hair and blue eyes. But they were such close friends that they were almost like sisters. They both wanted to be singing stars when they grew up.

"Hi, Holly," they both said at once. "Hi," Holly said. She handed them each a flyer. "I'm having a meeting at my house today. We need to save Peterson Park."

Holly told them about the mayor's plan to destroy the park.

"That's terrible!" Grace said.

"I'm sure my mom will let me come," Taylor added.

Holly smiled. "Great! See you then."

Holly passed out the rest of the flyers. Everyone seemed interested in helping to save the park!

I hope Mom has enough cookies in the house, Holly thought.

Chapter Four

Save the Bark?

"Where is everybody?" Holly asked.

"We're right here," Zachary said.

Holly, Zachary, Grace, and Taylor were sitting around Holly's kitchen table. A big pile of flower-shaped cookies sat in front of them on a plate.

"I mean everybody *else*," Holly said with a frown. "I thought we'd have lots and lots of people here to help save the park."

Just then, the doorbell rang. Holly jumped up.

"I'll get it!" she said. She raced to the front door and looked through the tiny window.

Anna, a girl from her class, stood on the front step with her mom behind her. Holly was surprised to see her. Anna was the quietest girl in class.

Holly opened the door.

"Hi," she said.

"Hi," Anna said shyly. Her mom gave her a hug, and Anna followed Holly into the kitchen.

"Hi, Anna!" Grace said, waving. Anna smiled, looking down at her shoes. Her brown bangs hung over her eyes.

"Let's get started," Holly said, sitting

down at the table. "We have a lot to do."

"I thwink woosh shoos hab a paddy," Zachary said. His mouth was full of cookies.

"What?" Holly asked.

Zachary swallowed and brushed the crumbs from his mouth. "We should have a big party in the park!"

"Ooh, that would be fun!" Taylor said. "Grace and I could sing a song in the gazebo for the crowd. We've been practicing."

But Holly had her own idea. "A party will take too long to put together," she said. "I know something we can do today. We can have a parade!"

Zachary looked confused. "With drums and flags and fire trucks?"

"Of course not!" Holly said. "We'll make a big sign. Then Jessica will take us to the park so we can march around."

Zachary shrugged. "Okay. If that's what you want to do."

Holly yelled, "Jessica! Did Aunt Amy bring the art supplies?"

Jessica poked her head into the kitchen. "They're in the backyard."

Holly and her friends went outside. A long piece of white paper as big as a door was lying on the grass. Small plastic bottles of paint and paintbrushes were neatly stacked to one side.

"Ooh, paint!" Grace said, her eyes lighting up. She picked up a bottle of purple paint.

"Grace, you and Taylor should do the words because you have the nicest handwriting," Holly said. "The sign should say 'Save the Park' in green paint."

Grace frowned. "Can't I use purple?"

Holly shook her head. "The park is green. The sign has to be like the park."

She turned to Zachary and Anna. "Zachary, you can paint a tree on that side," she said, pointing to the sign. "Anna, you can paint some flowers underneath the tree. And I'm going to paint a bluebird on the other side."

Holly had been dreaming about the sign all day. In her head, she knew just what it should look like.

Grace sighed and gave the purple paint to Anna. "Here, you can use this for the flowers."

Everyone got to work. It took Holly a long time to paint the bird. She wanted to make sure it looked just like the bird in the park. After a while she noticed that Grace, Taylor, Zachary, and Anna were all standing around her.

"Are you done yet?" Zachary asked. "I have to be home for dinner soon."

"Yeah, me, too," Taylor added.

"All right, all right," Holly said. She painted one more feather on the bluebird's tail. Then she jumped up. "I'll go get Jessica. You guys bring the sign out front."

Holly ran inside. "Jessica? We're ready to go to the park now!" she yelled.

Jessica was reading a book on the couch. "Mom's going to owe me extra allowance," she said, rolling her eyes and getting to her feet. "You could at least say please."

"Please?" Holly asked sweetly.

"All right," Jessica said, following Holly through the front door.

Out front, Holly took one end of the sign, and Zachary took another. Grace, Taylor, and Anna marched behind them.

Jessica made a face. "Oh, great! Could this be any more embarrassing?"

Holly didn't let Jessica bother her. She felt excited as they walked down to the park. She noticed some people looking at the sign as they passed by. It was working!

Jessica stepped in front of the group to lead them across the street. When she got to the other side, she shook her head.

"I don't get it," she said. "Why does your sign say 'Save the *Bark*'?"

"No, it says 'Save the Park'!" Holly explained.

Then Holly took a good look at the sign. Jessica was right! The sign said SAVE THE BARK. She didn't notice it before, because she was in such a hurry.

"Oh, no!" Holly wailed.

The sign was all wrong!

Chapter Five

The Evil Queen

"Don't look at me," Taylor said. "Grace painted that word."

"I did not!" Grace said. "You did it."

Taylor and Grace started to argue. Holly felt terrible. Her friends were fighting, and her whole plan was ruined!

"It's not so bad," Anna said in a small voice, patting Holly's arm.

"Yeah," Zachary agreed. "Maybe nobody will notice."

Holly shook her head. "We have to go home."

Tweet tweet tweet!

Holly heard the little bluebird before she saw him. He landed on a nearby tree branch.

Chirp chirp chirp!

The bird's pretty song made Holly feel better. It was almost like he was telling her not to be upset.

She looked at the sign again. Zachary's tree was nice. And Anna had painted some very pretty flowers.

"You're right!" she told them, grinning. "The sign is fine. A park has trees, and trees have bark. So if we save the park, we'll save the bark, too. Let's march!"

Jessica let her hair hang in front of her face so that none of her friends would recognize her. Then they all began to march down the park path.

"Save the park! Save the park!" Holly chanted.

Zachary, Grace, and Taylor joined in. Anna's face turned bright red.

As they marched down the main park path, a man walking a poodle came toward them.

"'Save the Bark'?" he asked. "Are you trying to save dogs?"

"No, we're trying to save the *park*," Holly explained.

The man shook his head. "I'm confused!"

Next, they marched past a two white-haired ladies on a park bench.

"Oh, look," one of the ladies said. "How cute. They're playing a game."

Holly stopped. "It's not a game. We're trying to save the park."

"But your sign says 'Save the Bark,'" the woman noted.

"Right," Holly said, nodding firmly. "We did that on purpose. We want to save the trees in the park. And trees have bark."

As they marched on, more people were confused by what they were doing. A few people asked them about the sign. They seemed interested to learn what was happening to the park.

Soon it was time to head back home. Back at Holly's house, her friends' parents were waiting to pick them up.

"Bye!" Holly said. "See you tomorrow."

Holly spotted her mom's car in the driveway. She ran inside, dragging the sign behind her.

"Mom, look!" she called. "We had a parade in the park. We're spreading the word!"

Holly skidded to a stop in the kitchen.

Her mom was watching the small TV that sat on the counter. On the screen, Mayor Morgan was talking into a microphone.

Mayor Morgan had shiny black hair that was slicked into a bun on the back of her head. She had a thin face and bright blue eyes. Holly thought she looked like an evil queen in a fairy tale.

"A new shopping center is just what Maple Grove needs," she was saying. "Not many people use Peterson Park. But everyone needs to shop."

"That's not fair!" Holly cried. "Lots of people use the park."

Holly's mom put an arm around her. "It's good that the story is on the news. More people will hear about it this way. Don't worry, we'll keep trying," she said. "Now why don't you help me make dinner?"

After she ate, Holly went to her room. She put on her flower headband and tried to think.

If Mayor Morgan was like an evil queen, only a princess could stop her. Thanks to Princess Power, they had spread the word around the park. But that wasn't enough. Holly knew they needed *more* Princess Power.

If Mayor Morgan didn't think enough people used the park, they had to do something really fun. Something lots of people would come to.

Holly jumped up. "I know!"

She ran out of her room. "Mom! Mom!" she yelled.

"What is it?" Mrs. Greenwood asked, as Holly found her in the kitchen.

"I have the best idea," she said. "We

have to do it this Saturday, before it's too late."

"Do what?" her mom asked.

"A picnic," Holly said. "We need to have a Princess Picnic in the park!"

Chapter Six

Muddy Princesses

"This is going to be the best Princess Picnic ever!" Holly said, looking around the park and smiling.

"Are you sure you don't want to move to the picnic area?" asked Aunt Amy. "We could use the tables there."

"I'm sure," Holly replied. "Under the willow tree is the perfect place."

Holly's mom had to work, so she couldn't come to the Princess Picnic. But

Holly didn't want to wait. So Aunt Amy had agreed to help.

Aunt Amy was the younger sister of Holly's mom. She was shorter than Mrs. Greenwood, with lots of curly hair. Today she wore a long green skirt with a puffy white blouse. A yellow flower peeked out from her curls. Holly thought she looked just like a real princess.

Holly had dressed up for the picnic, too. She wore her flower headband in her hair, of course, and her favorite green skirt with the ruffles on the bottom. On top she wore a tie-dyed T-shirt that Aunt Amy had helped her make. It had green swirls on it, and in glitter it said SAVE THE PARK.

"It *is* pretty here," Aunt Amy agreed. She looked up at the sky. "I just don't like those clouds. I hope it doesn't rain."

"It won't," Holly said firmly. Nothing

was going to ruin her Princess Picnic!

At that moment, the bluebird flew to the raspberry bush nearby and began to sing a happy song.

"See?" Holly said. "The bluebird knows it's not going to rain."

Aunt Amy smiled.

"I like your attitude, Holly," she said. "Now let's set up this picnic!"

Holly helped Aunt Amy spread out a big green picnic blanket. They unpacked a cooler with lots of treats to eat. Earlier that morning, Aunt Amy had mixed up a big thermos of sparkling green punch. Holly's mom had made a bunch of tiny, tasty cucumber-and-cream-cheese sandwiches. And Holly had even made something all by herself: magic fruit wands. She cut up pieces of strawberries and bananas and stuck them on straws to make delicious princess wands.

Zachary arrived while Holly and Aunt
Amy were setting up.

"Hi!" he said. "Is it time to eat?"

"Zachary, you're always hungry!"
Holly said, giggling. She looked at her
friend. "What are you supposed to be?"

Zachary was wearing two rectangles
of cardboard covered in aluminum foil.
The rectangles were connected by strings
that went over his shoulders. He held a
cardboard sword covered with aluminum
foil, too.

"I am a Sir Zachary, the Knight of Peterson Park!" he announced, waving his sword in the air.

Aunt Amy picked up her green skirt and curtseyed. "Nice to meet you, Sir Zachary," she said. "If you're not too busy slaying dragons, maybe you can help us set up the games."

Zachary bowed. "At your service."

Before long, the rest of the princesses started showing up. Grace and Taylor came first. Grace wore a pink dress and a sparkly princess crown. Taylor wore a purple dress with a heart on the front.

"Oh, Holly, it's so pretty here," Taylor said.

"I've never even been to this part of the park," Grace added. "I usually just go on the swings."

Almost all of the girls from Holly's class came to the Princess Picnic with their moms and dads. Lots of the girls dressed like princesses. Anna had on a pretty white sundress.

Holly was happy to see everybody. But something was bothering her. "There should be more people here," she said. "We need lots and lots of people to get Mayor Morgan's attention."

Zachary shrugged. "Maybe not everybody likes princesses," he said.

"Or maybe they're afraid it will rain," said Taylor, looking at the sky.

"It is *not* going to rain," Holly insisted.

Aunt Amy made an announcement. "Okay, everyone, it's game time!"

Everyone gathered around Aunt Amy. Holly saw that Anna stayed back by the tree. Holly ran over and grabbed her hand.

"Come on, it'll be fun!" she said. "Aunt

Amy knows the best games."

First they played a game like hot potato, except they used a stuffed frog. They sat in a circle and passed the frog to each other until Aunt Amy yelled "Ribbit!" The person holding the frog had to leave the circle. They kept going until one person was left. Grace won!

Then they searched for treasure that Aunt Amy and Zachary had hidden around the park earlier. The girls cheered every time they found a shiny fake jewel or gold coin. In the end, Aunt Amy counted to see who found the most.

"Anna is the winner!" she announced.

Anna blushed bright red.

Holly couldn't wait for the next game. A castle-shaped piñata hung from the branch of an oak tree. But Aunt Amy was peering up at the sky. Dark clouds covered every spot of blue.

"I think we should eat now," she said. She sounded worried.

Holly looked over at the raspberry bush. The bluebird wasn't there anymore.

It will not rain! Holly said to herself. *It will not rain!*

The princesses and Zachary sat on the picnic blanket. They ate sandwiches and fruit wands, and drank sparkly punch. While they ate, Aunt Amy talked to the moms and dads about the park.

"Isn't this a great picnic?" Holly asked.

"It sure is," Zachary said. "Maybe we can have a big party next."

Then a rumbling sound rolled across the park.

"It's thunder!" Taylor squealed.

"No!" Holly cried. "It can't rain!"

But it did, and it happened fast. The

clouds opened up and dumped buckets of rain down on the park.

The girls laughed and screamed as they jumped up from the picnic blanket.

"Quick! Let's pack everything up!" Aunt Amy yelled.

Everyone pitched in. They rolled up the picnic blanket. Their shoes squished on the muddy ground.

Then Holly remembered the castle piñata. It was going to be ruined if they didn't get it out of the tree quickly.

"The piñata!" she shouted.

Zachary ran to grab it—and slipped in the mud! He went down with a splash. "Help!" he yelled.

Grace and Taylor ran to grab his arms and pick him up. But they both slipped in a muddy patch, too!

"My new dress!" Taylor cried.

Grace started to giggle.

"What's so funny?" Taylor yelled.

Holly couldn't believe it. The Princess Picnic should have been the best picnic in the world. But the castle piñata was ruined. The sandwiches were soggy. And all of the princesses were wet and muddy!

How am I supposed to save the park now? Holly wondered.

Chapter Seven

The Mystery Note

Back at home, Holly changed out of her wet clothes. Mrs. Greenwood was home from her meeting. She wrapped Holly in a nice warm quilt while Aunt Amy made hot cocoa.

"Mom, did you tell Mayor Morgan about the Princess Picnic?" Holly asked.

"Yes, I did," her mom replied. "She said it sounded very nice. But it didn't change her mind."

Holly felt frustrated. "No matter what I do, it doesn't make any difference," she said sadly.

"That's not true," said Mrs. Greenwood. "Holly, you are trying very hard. But you're just a little girl. You shouldn't feel like you have to save the park all by yourself."

"But nobody else cares," Holly mumbled in a grumpy voice.

"Aunt Amy and I care," her mom said. "And so do Zachary and Grace and Taylor and Anna."

"And those people who came to the park today," Aunt Amy added, handing Holly a mug of hot cocoa with marshmallows. "Maybe you just need to slow down and listen to your friends. They might have good ideas. Didn't Zachary say something about a party?"

"But I like my ideas better!" Holly said stubbornly. "Besides, we have to hurry before the park gets torn down. A big party would take forever to put together!"

Mrs. Greenwood stroked Holly's brown hair. The ends of her braids were frizzy from the rain. "If I were you, I would take a deep breath and count to ten, my princess," she said. "We won't give up, I promise."

Holly nodded. She took a deep, deep breath. Then she let it out with a *whoosh*!

"Good girl," said Mrs. Greenwood.

Holly managed to forget about the park for the rest of the night. Aunt Amy stayed over, and they watched a movie and played board games. Even Jessica joined in! But the next morning, after Aunt Amy left, Holly couldn't help thinking about the park again.

She sat on the front steps with her chin in her hands.

Jessica poked her head out of the front door. "I'm going to the park," she said. "Do you want to come?"

"Really?" Holly asked. Her eyes narrowed. "How much is Mom paying you?"

"Nothing," Jessica said. "I just feel like going, okay? You don't have to come if you don't want to."

Holly jumped up. "I definitely want to come!" she said. "Let's go!" She wanted to spend as much time as possible in her favorite place . . . while she still could.

Holly felt better as soon as the park

came into sight. "Can we go to the willow tree?" she asked.

"Of course," Jessica said. "Where else would we go?"

The sunny morning had dried up all of the mud from the day before. Best of all, the bluebird was back. He darted from branch to branch on the willow tree. The branches gently waved up and down.

"Look, he's saying hello!" Holly said. She held up her finger. "Here, little bluebird. Come sit on my finger!"

The bluebird flew a little bit closer to Holly and settled on a branch in the middle of the willow tree. Holly slowly took one step, then another. Soon, she was so close she could almost touch him.

Chirp chirp!

The bluebird flew away.

"Come back!" Holly called out.

She was sad for a second. Then she

noticed something sticking out of the bark on the willow tree's trunk. It was a folded green piece of paper.

"What's this?" Holly wondered out loud.

She carefully slid the paper out. Her name was written on the front of the note!

"It's for me!" she cried.

"What does it say?" Jessica asked. Her green eyes twinkled.

Holly read the note to her sister.

Dear Holly,
Please come to the park next
Saturday with your mom, Aunt
Amy, and Jessica at 1:00. You will
get a special surprise.

Holly looked at Jessica. "A surprise?" she asked. "Did you write this?"

Jessica shook her head. "Nope. I guess we'll have to find out next Saturday."

Holly felt really excited. How could she possibly wait that long?

Chapter Eight

Party in the Park

Holly woke up super early on Saturday. The morning seemed to last forever! Holly tried to keep busy. She cleaned her room. She helped her mom fold laundry. She read a book and ate a sandwich for lunch.

When it was almost time to go, Holly put on her flower headband. Then she grabbed her mother's hand.

"Come on," she said. "It's time!"

"You're right," said Mrs. Greenwood. "You look very pretty, by the way. Just like a true princess."

Holly nodded. "I don't know what the surprise is, but I think some Princess Power might come in handy."

"I think you're right." Holly noticed that her mom had a special smile on her face, like she knew a secret.

"Mom, do *you* know what the surprise is?" Holly asked.

"Not exactly," Mrs. Greenwood said. "There's only one way to find out."

Holly ran to the door. "Let's go!"

Aunt Amy was outside, waiting. Holly held tightly to her mom's hand as they walked a few blocks to the park. Jessica walked a little bit behind them. When they turned the corner, Holly gasped.

The park was filled with people! Plus,

there was a big sign over the park entrance that said SAVE THE PARK!

"What's going on?" Holly asked, her eyes wide. She couldn't believe what she was seeing.

"Maybe you should ask the official tour guide," Mrs. Greenwood said. She nodded to Zachary, who stood by the park entrance. He wore a baseball cap with a card on it that said TOUR GUIDE in big letters. Holly ran up to him.

"Zachary, did you do this?" she asked.

Zachary nodded. "I felt bad that it rained on your picnic," he said. "My uncle Ted is an ice-cream man. He loves the park, too. He said he'd give away free ice cream at the park today. He told everyone on his ice-cream route about it."

Holly saw the ice-cream truck down the street, not far away. A long line of

people stood next to it, waiting for their free ice cream.

Zachary nodded to the gazebo. "Grace and Taylor are going to sing later," he said.

Holly couldn't believe it. "This is awesome!" she said. "But why didn't you tell me?"

"I wanted to surprise you," Zachary said. Then he looked down at his sneakers. "Besides, I wasn't sure if you'd let us do it."

Zachary sounded a little bit sad. Holly remembered what her mom said about listening to her friends. She hadn't listened to Zachary at all. Or Grace. Or Taylor.

"I'm sorry I didn't listen before," Holly said. "It's a really good idea."

A grin stretched over Zachary's face. "Thanks!" he said. He reached into his backpack and pulled out another baseball cap. This one said TOUR GUIDE on it, too. "Here's one for you."

"Cool!" Holly said. "What are we supposed to do?"

"I thought we could give people tours of the park," Zachary answered. "We could show them our favorite places. Then they would understand why the park is so special."

"That's a great idea!" Holly agreed. "Can we give my mom and Aunt Amy a tour?"

"Sure," Zachary said.

Holly found her mom talking to Anna's mom. Anna smiled and waved when she saw Holly and Zachary.

"Hey, Anna," Holly said. "What's your favorite place in the park?"

Anna thought for a bit. "I like the pond," she said.

Holly took off her tour guide hat and

put it on Anna's head. "You should give us a tour!"

Anna blushed. "I don't know what to say."

"Just tell us what you like about it," Holly said. She cupped her hands around her mouth. "Free tour of the park!

A small group of people formed around them. Holly and Zachary led the tour. Zachary talked about the playground, with its swings and slides and jungle gym. Holly talked about her favorite trees and flowers. And when they got to the pond, Anna talked about how she liked to watch the fish and the frogs there.

The party was a lot of fun—and a

big success! Grace and Taylor sang some songs in the gazebo. Everyone got free ice cream. Plus, Holly's mom and Aunt Amy had brought a special letter about saving the park. It was called a petition. They got lots of people to sign it.

"What a great party," Holly told Zachary. "Mayor Morgan can't ignore this!"

"Thanks," Zachary said. "But we've been so busy that we forgot one important thing."

"What?" Holly asked.

Zachary smiled. "It's our turn for free ice cream!"

Chapter Nine

The Bluebird of
Maple Grove

"I can't believe we got two hundred people to sign the petition," Holly said a few days later. "Mayor Morgan *has* to listen to us now!"

Holly carried the petition in a big yellow envelope. Jessica was taking her to town hall, where their mom worked. Mrs. Greenwood had said that they could give the petition to Mayor Morgan.

Holly was a little nervous. She had never met Mayor Morgan in person before. What if she really *was* an evil queen? She might turn Holly into a frog. Or trap her inside a magic mirror!

I will have to use Princess Power if that happens, Holly thought, trying to be brave.

"Earth to Holly? We're here," Jessica said, waving her hand in front of Holly's face.

They walked through the glass doors and down the hallway to their mother's office. Mrs. Greenwood was working on her computer. She got up and gave them both a hug.

"Come in and sit down for a minute," she said, closing the door behind her. "Holly, I have some news. Mayor Morgan is about to hold a press conference outside. She found someone who wants to buy the park."

Holly stood up. "But she can't! She hasn't seen our letter yet!"

"Nothing is final," her mom said. "I just want you to know the truth. We might not be able to save the park in the end."

"Yes we can!" Holly said firmly. "We just need to use Princess Power!"

"Princess *what*?" Jessica asked.

Mrs. Greenwood stood up. "Let's go outside to the press conference. We can give the letter to the mayor when it's over."

Holly's mom led them through the hallways. Maple Grove's town flag hung on a pole next to the mayor's office. The flag showed a maple tree with a bluebird flying on either side of it.

Holly stopped. "Mom, look!" she said. "That's the bluebird from the park!"

Mrs. Greenwood looked interested. "You mean the bird on the flag?"

Holly nodded.

"She talks to it all the time," Jessica added

"Holly, that's wonderful news!" Mrs. Greenwood said. "The Eastern bluebird is the town bird of Maple Grove. Years ago, the bluebirds went away because  people cut down trees and built houses. And now there's one in Peterson Park again!"

"That's good, right?" Holly asked.

Mrs. Greenwood nodded. "That bluebird is very important, Holly. We have to tell the mayor."

Holly was suddenly feeling very brave. "Let's tell her right now."

They headed outside to the press conference. Mayor Morgan stood on top of the stairs behind a microphone, and reporters stood on the steps below. They raised their hands and asked her lots of questions. Holly raised her hand, too.

But Mayor Morgan did not call on her. She talked a lot about selling the park. Then she said, "Now I have to get back to work."

"Hey, you didn't answer this reporter's question!" Jessica yelled out, pointing to Holly.

The reporters turned and spotted Holly behind them.

"Oh, isn't she cute?" said one of the reporters. "What's your question, little girl?"

Mayor Morgan stared at Holly with her icy blue eyes. For a second, Holly froze.

"Hurry up, please," Mayor Morgan said impatiently.

It's time for some Princess Power! Holly thought. She cleared her throat.

"Mayor Morgan," she said loudly. "Did you know that a bluebird lives in Peterson Park?"

"No, I didn't know that," Mayor Morgan replied, looking annoyed. "But one bird is not very important."

"But Mayor Morgan, the Eastern bluebird is the town bird of Maple Grove! They've been gone for years. Didn't you know that?" one of the reporters asked.

The mayor looked embarrassed. "Oh, um, of course I did," she replied.

Holly piped up again. "You think that everyone wants a shopping center, but they really want to save the park! I have a letter here that says so. It's signed by more than two hundred people!" She marched up to Mayor Morgan and handed her the yellow envelope.

The mayor cleared her throat, looking frazzled and confused. "This is all very sudden. I will have to look into this further."

"Does that mean the sale of the park is on hold?" a reporter pressed.

"Yes!" Mayor Morgan snapped. "No more questions!" With that, she turned and walked back into the town hall.

Holly's mom hugged her as the reporters turned to take Holly's picture. "Great job, Holly!" she said.

Jessica ruffled Holly's hair. "Not bad, little sister."

Holly couldn't believe she had been brave enough to talk to the mayor. Could the park really be saved?

Chapter Ten

A Real Princess

"You did it, Holly!" Zachary cheered. "You saved the park!"

"We *all* did it," Holly told him. "Everybody helped. Without your party, we never would have gotten all those people to sign the petition. But most of all, the bluebird did it."

Holly and her friends were playing under the willow tree a few days after the press conference. Grace and Taylor were

practicing some dance steps. Anna was
quietly reading a book.

The little bluebird flew to a branch of
the willow tree to watch them. Grace and
Taylor stopped dancing.

"Look, there he is!" Zachary
whispered.

*Tweet tweet tweet tweet tweet! Chirp chirp
chirp!*

Holly held out her hand. "Come here,
little bird," she said in a sweet voice. "I

want to thank you for saving the park."

The bluebird flew toward Holly . . . and landed right on the end of her finger! Holly held her breath.

Chirp chirp! the bird said in greeting. Then he flew away.

Everyone stared at Holly.

"Wow," said Zachary.

"That was amazing!" Grace added.

"He really landed on your finger!" Taylor squealed.

"Holly, that's just like something that would happen to a *real* princess," Anna said softly.

Holly smiled.

She *felt* just like a real princess, too!

Make It Yourself!
Princess Flower Headband

You don't have to live near a park like Holly to enjoy beautiful flowers every day. Make this flower crown to become the princess of your very own garden!

Level of difficulty: Medium
(You'll need some help from a grown-up.)

You need:

- 1 plastic headband, any color
- 2 sheets of felt in different colors
- scissors
- fabric glue

1. Cut the felt into 7 flower shapes like the one on this page.
2. Using the other color felt, cut out a small circle for the middle of each flower.
3. With the fabric glue, stick one circle to each flower.
4. Glue each flower to the plastic headband, with one in the middle and three on each side. (You can also use a hot glue gun for this part, but you **must** have a grown-up help you.)
5. Wait for the flowers to dry—then wear your crown!

Don't miss another royal
adventure—look for

Orange Princess

Has a

Ball

Turn the page for
a special sneak peek!

Kristina Kim climbed down the steps of the school bus. Grandma Soo was waiting by the front door of their house, just like she did every day.

Kristina raced down the walk. She waved a piece of orange paper in her hand.

"Grandma Soo! Grandma Soo, look!" she cried.

Peter, her younger brother, ran past her. He gave Grandma Soo a big hug. Then he turned and stuck his tongue out at Kristina.

"Ha! I beat you!" he said.

"Peter, be nice to your big sister," Grandma Soo said. "Now go inside and wash your hands. There is some fruit on the table if you're hungry."

Peter ran inside.

"Grandma Soo, there's going to be a real ball!" Kristina said. She held out the piece of paper. "Everyone in school is invited. We get to wear costumes. And there will be music and dancing and—"

"Slow down, Kristina," Grandma Soo said with a smile. "I see that you are excited, but it is chilly out here. Come inside and tell me more."

Kristina *was* very excited. But she followed her grandmother inside. She always listened to Grandma Soo! Kristina hung her orange backpack on a hook in the hallway. She put her sweater in the closet. Peter's backpack and jacket were on the floor.

On another day, Kristina would have told on Peter. But not today. She wanted to talk about the ball! She followed Grandma Soo into the kitchen.

"Read it, Grandma," Kristina said, handing her grandmother the orange sheet of paper. "It tells all about the ball."

Grandma Soo read the invitation.

"*A Fall Ball*," Grandma Soo read. "That sounds like a nice party."

"It's not just a party, it's a *ball!*" Kristina corrected her. "Just like in a fairy tale, with dancing and everything. And I get to wear a costume! Can you guess what I'll be?"

Grandma Soo's dark eyes twinkled. "Let me think. You will be . . . a cowgirl?" Kristina put her hands on her hips. "No, Grandma!"

"Hmm. A witch?" Grandma asked.

Kristina shook her head. "No!"

"Maybe you will be a ghost, then," Grandma Soo said.

"Grandma! You *know* what I'm going to dress up as," Kristina told her. "A princess!"